MW01172606

BIGFOOT

SANTA

A Short Story

By

Scott M. Gano

Part 1

While making his daily travels through the forest,

Bigfoot, more often than he would like to admit, looked up

to the sky in search of Santa Claus. Being just over fifty-

years-old, an elderly age for the Sasquatch species, Bigfoot

once spotted Santa while enjoying the view of the moonlit

forest.

Normally, seeing such things like a plane or a

helicopter would make him retreat to avoid detection. He

was a pro at hiding. The Canadian Sasquatches were even

better. He hoped to one day be as good as they were. Now

Bigfoot had heard of Santa Claus before, but hearing those

sleigh bells and seeing Santa fly in his sleigh made Bigfoot lose his most basic instinct.

The first time Santa Claus appeared, he was gone within seconds. Immediately Bigfoot thought, *It's the Canadian Sasquatch!*

The thing that got ingrained into Bigfoot's mind that night was not Santa or his sleigh. It wasn't even the eight reindeer that flew through the air like they were running on solid ground. No. What impressed Bigfoot the most and made it an unforgettable night were the sparkling dust trails the sleigh left behind.

The dust trails reminded him of the Northern Lights he saw during his younger years. Instead of green trails they were bright red with what looked like sparkling stars inside. After a while the trails evaporated from the night sky and were gone.

Two years later on the same month, the same night, Bigfoot spotted Santa Claus again. While snacking on a few holly berries and sharing them with a friendly deer who allowed herself to be petted, Bigfoot noticed a faint jingling sound. His new deer-friend picked up the sound with her ears too, and began surveying the area with quick head movements. Bigfoot did the same. He then spoke in animal tongue. A language shared across the world within the animal kingdom.

"Did you hear that too?" Bigfoot asked.

"Yes," the deer whispered, her voice shaky.

"What do you think it was?"

The jingling sound came again. This time closer than before.

"Danger," the deer said. She turned and quickly galloped away.

Bigfoot stood his ground. He kept looking over his hairy shoulders. There was nothing in sight. Although his instincts were telling him to do what he does best and hide, another part of him said to stay put. Deciding to go against his instincts resulted in an unusual experience.

A large shadow ran through the moonlit forest. Bigfoot looked up to see a dark object, too large to be any kind of bird, flying over the tree line. Even with Bigfoot's nocturnal vision it was difficult to spot. The tall trees and the darkness of night worked together to block nearly all visibility. All that remained was the shadow running along the forest floor and every once in awhile the faint jingling sound in the crisp winter air.

The shadow moved fast and so did Bigfoot. He tracked it down in a sprint. Every which way the shadow went, he went as well. All of nature's animals and critters either watched from a safe distance or dashed away.

Bigfoot was a fast runner, but his strength to keep up slowly diminished. Being eight feet tall and roughly weighing over four-hundred pounds had its limits. As he felt the muscles throughout his legs burn and wear out, he did the next best thing to keep up with the shadow.

Pushing himself off the ground, he leaped seven feet into the air to latch onto the side of a tree trunk. Much of the bark broke off as he held on. More of it tore away when he launched himself higher to another tree. This time he reached his hand out for a thick branch and caught it. He swung himself and caught the next one. Keeping this momentum going, he swung from tree to tree, all the while staying with the shadow's pace from below.

Up ahead Bigfoot noticed glowing white and yellow lights. He knew these lights. They were a bad sign. Humans were close. He swung from the branch and landed back on his feet.

The shadow he chased never stopped. It soon disappeared from sight, heading straight towards a cluster of human dwellings. Bigfoot took a second to catch his breath before he crept to the edge of the forest. Hiding himself behind the trunk of a tree, he peeked an eye around the corner.

The neighborhood of glowing lights and homes were not what Bigfoot had his sights set on. As it turned out, the shadow belonged to the object he had seen two years ago. A sleigh and reindeer leaving a trail of red sparkling dust.

The sleigh landed on the roof of a house. Bigfoot then spotted a tall large being in a red suit hop out of the sleigh. He had no idea that Santa was a rare sight to see just like himself. But Bigfoot couldn't take his eye off him. He watched the man take a heavy red sack out of the sleigh and make his way toward the chimney. Right then, Bigfoot gasped.

The man's entire form suddenly turned into a red sparkling dust cloud before going down into the chimney.

Bigfoot no longer peeked one eye out from the side of the tree. He now poked his whole head to the side, waiting to see what would happen next.

Just as quickly as it had disappeared, the cloud of red dust reappeared. And once it was out, it quickly went down the next chimney. Then the one after that. Within minutes it managed to go down every chimney in the entire community. When the red dust cloud returned to the sleigh on the roof of the first home, it transformed back into the large red suited man. Once he was back in the sleigh, the reindeer were ready for takeoff.

Bigfoot grunted, "Wow" as the sleigh and reindeer flew over his head back to the forest. He moved quickly and gave chase again. This time he was able to keep up. Not just because his legs had rested, but because the sleigh moved at a much slower pace above the trees. This made him wonder why their speed had dropped so dramatically. The reason came from a groaning sound Bigfoot picked up on. A sound of pain coming from one of the flying reindeer.

He slowed his pace when he saw the reindeer begin their descent. They made a swift landing on the side of a two-lane road paved through the dense forest. Bigfoot listened to his instincts this time and hid behind the closest tree available. When a few seconds passed, he peeked around the corner.

Not much could be seen from his point of view. He stood nearly six yards away with thick tree trunks and brush between him and the road. He took a chance and decided to move in for a better look. As he did this, he noticed the man step out of the sleigh and check on the disgruntled reindeer. Not only did the man clad in a red suit and hat appear just as tall as him, Bigfoot's small ears perked up the moment he heard him actually speak in animal tongue.

"You doing okay, Comet," Santa asked, petting the reindeer's back while Comet sniffled and whined.

"Catching a cold, huh. Luckily we managed to finish early

this year. Let's try to head back home. I'm sure the Misses

will want to take good care of you."

Bigfoot quickly realized he had overstepped his

bounds. He had snuck in close to hear the man speak. Way

too close. Bigfoot attempted to correct this one mistake by

stepping back to leave.

Snap!

A lone twig broke in half under the pressure of his

big foot.

The entire forest suddenly fell silent. Bigfoot and

Santa were now face to face. Eye to eye. Both of them

stood at the same height at almost the same stature.

Bigfoot of course had more muscle, whereas Santa had

more fat.

"He does exist…" Santa said before his eyes rolled

back and his body collapsed in a faint.

Part 2

All eight reindeer witnessed the whole thing.

Bigfoot thought that he could not feel any more

embarrassed. What made it worse though were some of the

reindeer's comments.

"Good job, Big man," Comet said, sarcastically.

"Look what you did, Stinky!" Donner mocked.

"He killed Santa Claus!" Prancer cried.

Apparently, Bigfoot could feel more embarrassed.

He stepped out of the woods, revealing his full form. None

of Santa's reindeer reacted appalled, frightened, or excited to see a Sasquatch for the first time. Their focus, as well as Bigfoot's, remained on Santa and nothing else.

Bigfoot kneeled next to Santa and hovered his large hand over the man's face. When warmth hit the center of his palm, his nerves immediately felt some relief.

"He's okay," he said. "He's still breathing."

"Oh, praise the Spirit of Christmas," Prancer said.

Bigfoot shook his head, still reeling from embarrassment and regret. "Look, I am so sorry. If there's anything I can do to make this right, please tell me."

"What could you possibly do?" Blitzen sassed.

"He could help us take Santa back home," Vixen said. "Even if all eight of us worked together, there's no way we can lift him in or out of the sleigh by ourselves."

Bigfoot did not waste any more time. He scooped

Santa off the ground with ease and gently placed him in

the back of the sleigh.

All eight reindeer stared at him with big eyes and

hanging jaws. Blitzen was the first to shake himself out of

the stunned moment and speak.

"How the heck did you—"

"Let's get a move on," Dasher yelled.

Bigfoot stepped into the sleigh. Once seated, the

reindeer were off. They rose with a jingle, red dust coming

off their hooves and the bottom of the sleigh. It took a

moment for Bigfoot to gain his balance from the take off.

Once he did, he peeked over the edge to see they were

already high over the trees.

Staring down from this height and still climbing into the starry night sky shocked his senses. He let out a howl of fear and panic. One of the eight reindeer laughed at him. They entered the clouds and came out on the other side where the glowing face of the giant moon greeted them. All the fear and panic Bigfoot felt had been washed away. For just a few short seconds he soaked in the sight of the moon before the reindeer made a sudden stop.

Like a roller coaster, the reindeer reached their maximum altitude. Then they galloped in a decline, heading back into the thick layer of clouds. When they passed through, the scenery changed dramatically.

The giant forest and small town of humans Bigfoot knew were gone. This was a new place. A colder place with falling snow and a smaller town-like area with

brighter and more colorful lights.

"What is this," Bigfoot hollered to make sure the

reindeer heard him. "Where are we?"

Comet sneezed and shook his antlers before

answering. "We're in the North Pole. And that there is

Santa's Workshop, known to us and the elves as

Winterland."

Bigfoot tried to get a good look at Winterland, but

there was too much wind and snow to see clearly. Even

when the reindeer made their landing, there was no time to

look around. The sleigh kept moving, passing what looked

like streetlights and multiple decorated fir trees. As they

approached a giant barn-like structure, the reindeer slowed

their pace. The front of the structure had three floors of brightly lit frosted windows and two large wood paneled doors. The doors opened as the reindeer entered with Santa and Bigfoot.

Bigfoot was awestruck. There were elves the size of human children and strange running machinery everywhere. Some elves were pushing carts filled with rolls of dazzling wrapping paper, toys, and decorations. Others sorted through piles of sweet-scented candy. As the reindeer pulled the sleigh through the workshop, more and more elves stopped and stared with dropped jaws and big eyes, just as interested in Bigfoot, apparently, as he was in them.

"Not to worry everyone," Donner assured the elves. "Santa is with us. He's okay. Not to worry. We just have a giant Sasquatch onboard."

The reindeer made their way to the back of the workshop. Once the reindeer and sleigh came to a stop, a voice spoke up.

"Comet, Cupid, where is my husband?"

The voice belonged to Mrs. Claus. A woman in a red gown and long wavy white hair with a royal blue streak. She gasped and her eyes grew once she saw Santa passed out in the back of the sleigh.

"Nicholas," she exclaimed, shaking his shoulder. "Darling, what happened to you?" Her focus then moved to the front of the sleigh. She crept forward. Mrs. Claus was taken aback at the harsh stench of the creature, but resolved to keep her composure. Bigfoot looked at Mrs. Claus and with mighty caution stood at his full height.

"Mrs. Claus, meet Bigfoot," Comet said.

Bigfoot could see she was in shock. Those who were lucky enough to catch a glimpse of his existence often are. But then something happened. A smile took over the look of surprise along with tears. These were not ones of fear, but tears of joy.

Bigfoot stepped out of the sleigh, shyness overtaking him in the presence of the beautiful woman. A blush spread across his cheeks, partially hidden by the fur on his face.

Mrs. Claus laughed and wiped away a tear. She then spoke in animal tongue. "I never stopped believing."

Not knowing what to say or do, Bigfoot put on a smile of his own. Before he could say anything, Mrs. Claus turned to the reindeer. "Where did he come from?"

After the reindeer explained, and understanding full well that in no way could they have gotten Santa back to Winterland on their own, Mrs. Claus asked a favor of her own. "If you wouldn't mind, could you carry my husband to bed?"

Bigfoot looked to Santa, then back to Mrs. Claus. "Yes," he replied.

Mrs. Claus smiled again. After Bigfoot lifted Santa out of the sleigh and over his shoulder, he followed Mrs.

Claus into a luxurious bedroom. One side of the room had a fireplace with two leather chairs. The other had a king-size bed with a decorated wood headboard and footboard. Mrs. Claus pointed toward the bed and Bigfoot carefully laid him down.

"Thank you," she said. "Thank you for all your assistance. I've tried to get him to hire more help, but he can be overconfident of himself at times."

Bigfoot had no idea how to respond. Instead, he decided to standby till he could be of use.

"Have you ever been given a Christmas present before?"

Not knowing how to answer, or what a Christmas present even was, Bigfoot remained silent. Mrs. Claus, though, could not wait. She went to the fireplace and took

something hanging off one of the chairs. She returned with

it and said, "Could you kneel for me, please."

Getting down on one knee felt awkward and strange.

When Bigfoot did this, Mrs. Claus guided his arms through

the open areas of a garment. "There," she said, smiling. "I

knew it would be a perfect fit. Let's take a look in the

mirror." She then took his hand and led him to a large

mirror on the wall. "What do you think?"

Bigfoot let his hands roam across the brown coat,

noting the beige fur trim. It felt soft and warm. His hands

jumped as he let out a gasp. *This is animal fur*, he thought.

This feels like animal fur!

Mrs. Claus held his hand. "It's okay. It's not real. It's just an imitation to fur." She pointed to the mirror. "Take a look here."

Hearing this calmed Bigfoot's nerves. He took a step forward until he saw something in the mirror. A reflection of Mrs. Claus. Next, something more shocking. A reflection of himself wearing a coat. It did not occur to him that he was in fact seeing his own reflection until after a couple taps on the glass and a few face muscle movements.

"Do you like it?" Mrs. Claus asked.

Bigfoot focused back on the coat. He liked the comfort it offered. He knew it would be perfect for those winter nights when it's the coldest. He faced Mrs. Claus with a grin and nodded.

"It's one of my husband's coats. He barely wears it anymore. I want you to have it."

Bigfoot smiled. "Thank you."

Soon after, Mrs. Claus wished Bigfoot a Merry Christmas and sent him with the elves back to the sleigh. He got in and was flown back to his home in the forest within minutes. From then on he wore the coat as often as he could. Memories of his trip to Winterland consumed his thoughts and dreams.

Part 3

For an entire year, Bigfoot found himself looking to the sky in search of Santa Claus. He had told nearly every animal in the forest about his adventure. The brown coat alone proved his story to be true.

On the last day before Christmas Eve, Bigfoot had visitors waiting just outside his cave. His eyes widened as he grinned. Mrs. Claus waved at Bigfoot as she let the eight reindeer loose from the sleigh to wander.

"There you are," she said. "I was concerned we weren't going to find you here. Luckily Donner knew your scent and was able to track you." Mrs. Claus paused for a moment and smiled. "I see you're still wearing the coat."

Bigfoot nodded. "Yes. Thank you."

"You're welcome. Listen, this may sound strange but the reason I came looking for you is because I have another favor to ask."

Bigfoot's ears perked up. He stood straighter, ready and willing to help in any way he could.

"You see, my husband is still resting after running into you last year. I think the toll of the job as Santa has finally caught up to him after seventeen-hundred years. Anyways, what I wanted to ask is… would you be willing to fill in for Santa this Christmas?"

Without hesitation Bigfoot agreed.

Mrs. Claus smiled from ear to ear. "Thank you," she said gratefully.

Soon after, they hopped in the sleigh and took flight to the North Pole. Mrs. Claus urged the reindeer to hurry as there was still a lot of prepping to do before Christmas. All of the reindeer pushed themselves to go faster. To climb up through the clouds then back down. They reached the North Pole, coming in for a landing in Winterland and making their stop inside the workshop.

Inside, the elves were active. More so than the last time Bigfoot was here. Their movements were fast-paced and precise. They were pushing cartloads and carrying boxes of wrapped presents. Seeing them this way made

Bigfoot feel uncomfortable and nervous. That feeling

dissipated the moment Mrs. Claus took his hand.

"It's okay," she said. "Follow me."

Once they stepped out of the sleigh, Mrs. Claus gave

directions to the elves in their own language. Bigfoot could

not understand a word of it. Moments later Bigfoot found

himself sitting in a barber chair getting scrubbed, rinsed,

and combed. The only thing keeping him sane was Mrs.

Claus's presence and her persistent hold on his hand.

Next, the elves moved him to the fitting room. They

took his measurements and pulled multiple selections of

red suits. None seemed to catch his interest except for one.

"Excellent choice," Mrs. Claus said. "It matches your coat perfectly. And look, it even goes with this Santa hat."

Bigfoot tried on the hat with the suit and his coat. Now being used to seeing himself in the mirror, he felt quite pleased.

"Perfect," Mrs. Claus said. "Now let's get you some boots."

Bigfoot tried on multiple pairs of boots, none of them feeling quite right. His frustration at the confining objects finally elicited a growl.

"That's okay," Mrs. Claus assured him. "We will forgo the boots and you can go barefoot."

Bigfoot grunted in agreement.

Just then, Santa entered the fitting room.

"What in the Yeti! So the rumors are true," he said, holding his balance with a hand on the wall. "Bigfoot has come to town." He turned to Mrs. Claus. "But why? Why did you bring him? And why is he wearing my clothes?"

"I've been telling you for decades to take a break. And honestly, who else could literally fit into your suit?"

Santa Claus sighed. "Well, Sasquatch or not I'm still going. At least as a driver. Not once have I missed Christmas and I'm sure as a nutcracker not starting now. I will go as a Helper."

With that decided, Bigfoot and Santa suited up and headed out. Santa took the front seat of the sleigh while Bigfoot climbed in the back. Once the eight reindeer were strapped in and Santa's big red bag was squished in against

Bigfoot, the warehouse doors opened and they were off.

Pretty soon they were in the clouds and already descending

back down.

Bigfoot and Santa quickly got to work. Santa had to

walk Bigfoot through the process of delivering gifts. It felt

strange at first to deliver presents the way Santa did. Going

down the chimney with the bag, filling the stockings, and

placing the presents under the tree. After the third house

though, it became easy. He even started to enjoy it. And if

there were any cookies and milk left out, he brought it

back up for Santa to have. He especially enjoyed the

homes that were kind enough to leave a basket of whole

carrots addressed to the reindeer. He would feed each of

the reindeer, except for Comet who would offer his share

back to Bigfoot.

With bellies full and all the gifts delivered across the

globe, Santa guided the sleigh back to Bigfoot's home

nestled deep in the forest.

"Goodbye Bigfoot," Santa said. "Merry Christmas!

And thank you for all that you've done. Mrs. Claus and I

will never forget it."

"See ya later, fur-ball," Comet said.

Bigfoot smiled and waved as Santa and his sleigh

lifted into the air and flew away. When they were gone and

out of sight, Bigfoot took a moment to admire the starry

night sky before retiring to his cave. He then noticed a

small sparkling red dust trail rush past him and enter his

cave. He gasped with excitement and surprise and hurried inside.

There he found the red dust cloud hovering next to the spot where he normally sleeps. Soon the dust cloud dissolved into something whole. A large weaved basket filled with berries and carrots. From that moment on, every Christmas morning, Bigfoot would wake up to special gifts waiting just for him.

Bigfoot loved Christmas.

The End

Made in the USA
Columbia, SC
02 November 2023

25125346R00021